DISNEY ENCANTO

Adapted by
Naibe Reynoso

Illustrated by
Alejandro Mesa

Designed by
Tony Fejeran

🦋 A GOLDEN BOOK • NEW YORK

Copyright © 2021 Disney Enterprises, Inc. All rights reserved. Published in the United States by Golden Books, an imprint of Random House Children's Books, a division of Penguin Random House LLC, 1745 Broadway, New York, NY 10019, and in Canada by Penguin Random House Canada Limited, Toronto, in conjunction with Disney Enterprises, Inc. Golden Books, A Golden Book, A Little Golden Book, the G colophon, and the distinctive gold spine are registered trademarks of Penguin Random House LLC.

rhcbooks.com

ISBN 978-0-7364-4235-0 (trade) — ISBN 978-0-7364-4236-7 (ebook)

Printed in the United States of America

10 9 8 7 6 5

In a small village deep in the wilderness, an ever-glowing candle shone brightly.

Its magic was so powerful, a place of wonder was born . . . an Encanto!

The Madrigal family lived there in a home they called Casita.

The magic blessed all the Madrigals with **special gifts.**

Julieta could heal people with food.

Luisa had superstrength.

Isabela could make flowers grow.

Antonio could communicate with animals.

And Bruno could see the future.
But nobody talked about Bruno. He had been gone for many years.

When Mirabel was five years old, she got to wear her
special party dress! She and Abuela Alma were so
excited to find out what her gift was!

But when Mirabel touched the knob of her glowing door . . .
the magic went away!

She was the only Madrigal without a gift. This made her feel like she wasn't special enough or worthy enough.

One day, when Mirabel was fifteen, Casita started to crack.

It began to
shake.

"The house is in danger!" Mirabel cried.
Suddenly, she had an idea. If she found the reason
for the cracks, she could fix them and prove she was special!

Mirabel followed the cracks straight to the magical candle. Her sister Luisa told her that Bruno left the Encanto because of what he saw in his last vision about the future. Could it have something to do with the cracks?

Mirabel was determined to
find Bruno's **vision cave**.

After climbing endless stairs, she was finally inside his room.
There, she found glowing pieces of his **broken vision**.

Mirabel put all the pieces of Bruno's vision together. The puzzle revealed a destroyed Casita, and in the middle was MIRABEL!

What did it mean?

Meanwhile, more cracks started to ripple through the house. Mirabel was **running out of time!**

She discovered a **secret passageway** inside the walls. And there she found . . . Bruno! He had been living there the whole while!

Mirabel asked Bruno to look into the future. She believed it would help stop the cracks and restore Casita's magic!

Holding hands, they saw a doomed Casita,
the family pursued by dark cracks, and Mirabel standing
amidst the chaos.

Then . . . a glowing figure . . . it was ISABELA!

"Embrace her and you will see the way,"
said Bruno.

Mirabel thought Isabela was annoyingly perfect. But Isabela told her that she always felt she could never be perfect enough for Abuela.

Just then, the candle's light glowed brighter!

Abuela Alma was **angry** at all that Mirabel had been disrupting. She told Mirabel that the magic had started dying the day she didn't get a gift.

Mirabel had a **revelation:** The magic was dying because no one in the family was **ever good enough** for Abuela Alma!

Giant cracks appeared everywhere! The candle was almost completely **melted away**. The family members raced to save the candle, but their powers were fading.

In its last effort, Casita got Mirabel to safety.

Then

pooooffff...

The candle went out.
All the magic of Casita was gone!

Casita had **crumbled** into a pile of rubble and dust.
The entire Encanto shook. Everything was in **chaos**.

Feeling defeated, Mirabel ran away.

Mirabel wandered past the
mountains. At a nearby riverbank,
Abuela found her. It was the same place
where **the Encanto was born** and
Abuelo Pedro, Abuela's husband, was lost.

Abuela told Mirabel about that night long ago, how she
had **prayed for a miracle.** The candle's bright light
pushed back the bad men, protecting her and her triplets.

Losing Abuelo broke something inside Abuela that no magic flame could ever repair.

Since that day, Abuela felt that if the family was strong enough and worked hard enough, she could protect them. But now she realized her broken heart had made her live in fear.

"We were given a miracle because of you," Mirabel told Abuela.
This made Abuela feel better. "Mi vida . . . you are the
miracle," she told her granddaughter.

Bruno arrived at the river. Abuela hugged him. "I feel like I missed something important," he said.

"Come on," Mirabel said, and the three of them headed home.

Nobody could believe what they saw: Abuela, proudly walking alongside Mirabel and Bruno! Everyone realized what made them truly special wasn't their powers, it was their family bond—their love for one another.

They all worked together to rebuild Casita. There was just one last piece of the house left: the doorknob. As Mirabel placed it in the house . . .

WHOOSH!

Casita came back to life, and the Encanto's magic was restored. The family's gifts worked again!

And at last, Mirabel felt her OWN worth and her family's love.